Sticker Dolly Dressing
On Vacation

Lucy Bowman

Illustrated by Vici Leyhane,
Stella Baggott and Molly Sage

Contents

The back cover folds out so you
can "park" spare stickers there
while you dress the dolls.

Meet the dolls

Chloé, Megan and Tia are at the airport, waiting to board a plane and jet off. They love visiting exciting new places...

Chloé likes shopping and looking her best wherever she is in the world.

Megan loves sightseeing, and enjoys taking photos of all the places she visits.

Tia is sporty,
adventurous
and fun-loving.
She always
likes to be on
the go.

Tropical beach

On a beautiful tropical island, the dolls relax
on the golden sand, and swim and surf in the
warm blue ocean. When it gets too hot, they
eat delicious ice creams to cool down.

Skiing

In the snowy mountains, Megan, Chloé and Tia wrap up in layers of clothes to keep out the icy wind. After warming cups of hot chocolate at a lodge, the dolls are ready for action. Tia can't wait to jump onto her snowboard and swoosh down the slopes!

Skiing

On safari

The dolls are on a safari adventure. They've been driving over the African grasslands all morning and have spotted some amazing animals, including elephants, rhinos and zebras. Megan is very excited, as she's managed to take a photo of a cheetah in a tree.

Coral reef

Tia, Megan and Chloé have dived down into the magical world of a coral reef, filled with strange-shaped corals and underwater creatures. They've discovered scuttling crabs, shoals of fish, pretty shells and even a giant green turtle.

Taking photos

Megan is visiting the pyramids. It's a scorching hot day, so she wears long loose clothes to keep cool. She takes photos of the pyramids and a camel train as it treks across the sandy desert.

City shopping

Chloé is shopping for clothes in New York. The department stores have all the latest fashions. There's so much to choose from that she already has lots of bags to carry.

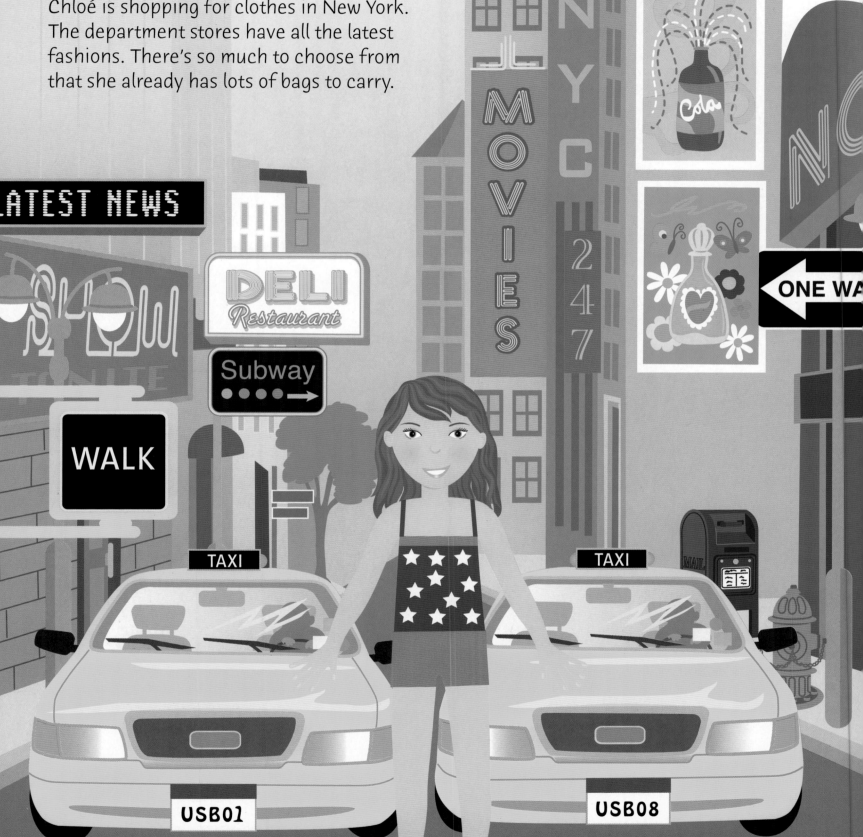

All aboard

It's a sunny day and there's a warm breeze blowing across the bay. Chloé, Tia and Megan are getting ready to set sail and join the dolphins splashing about in the clear blue water.

Mermaid

On the ranch

Down on the ranch, Chloé is about to saddle up and go for a ride across the grassy plains, while Tia and Megan are helping to feed the horses. After that, they're going to learn how to use a rope to lasso the cattle – soon they'll be real cowgirls!

Camping out

The dolls have found a pretty place to pitch their tents at a campsite. They will spend the day swimming in the lake and watching the birds in the trees, before tucking up for the night in their warm sleeping bags.

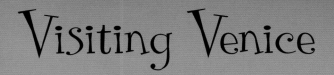

Visiting Venice

When it's carnival time in Venice, everyone wears mysterious masks and glamorous gowns. As fireworks light up the night sky, the dolls wait for gondolas to take them across the lagoon.

In the jungle

It's hot and humid in the rainforest. The air is filled with the strange noises of monkey calls and bird songs. The dolls are excited about exploring the lush jungle, and looking for amazing insects and animals hiding amongst the plants and trees.

Photo album

After their trips, the dolls look through all their photos. They put them in an album so they'll never forget all the amazing places they've visited.

Edited by Leonie Pratt. Series editor: Fiona Watt. This edition first published in 2020 by Usborne Publishing Ltd., 83-85 Saffron Hill, London, EC1N 8RT, England usborne.com

coral reef

Pages 10-11

Taking photos

city shopping

Page 12

Page 13

24 HOURS

BROADWAY

STOP

BIG APPLE

ZOOM

All aboard

Pages 14-15

On the ranch

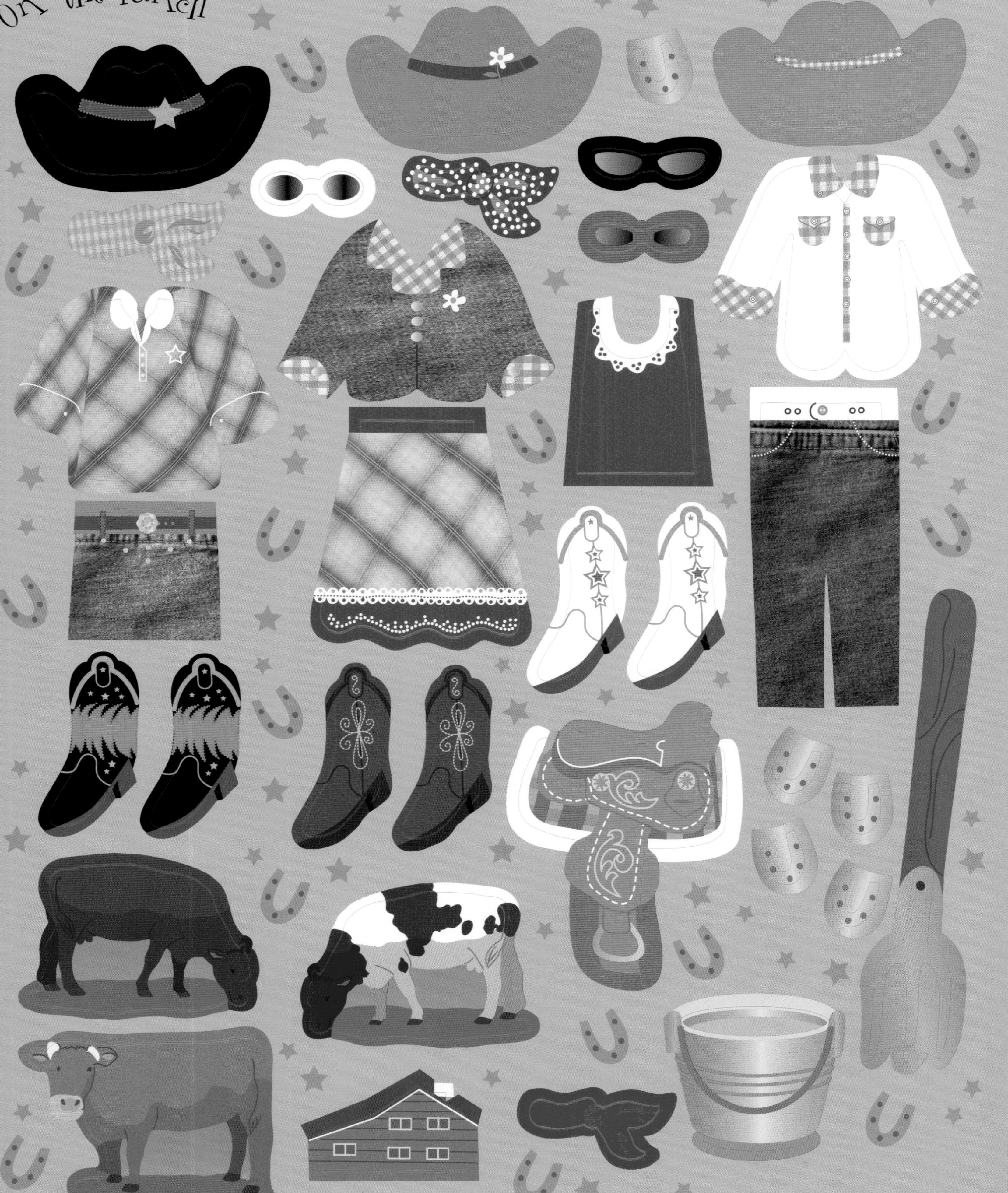

Pages 16–17

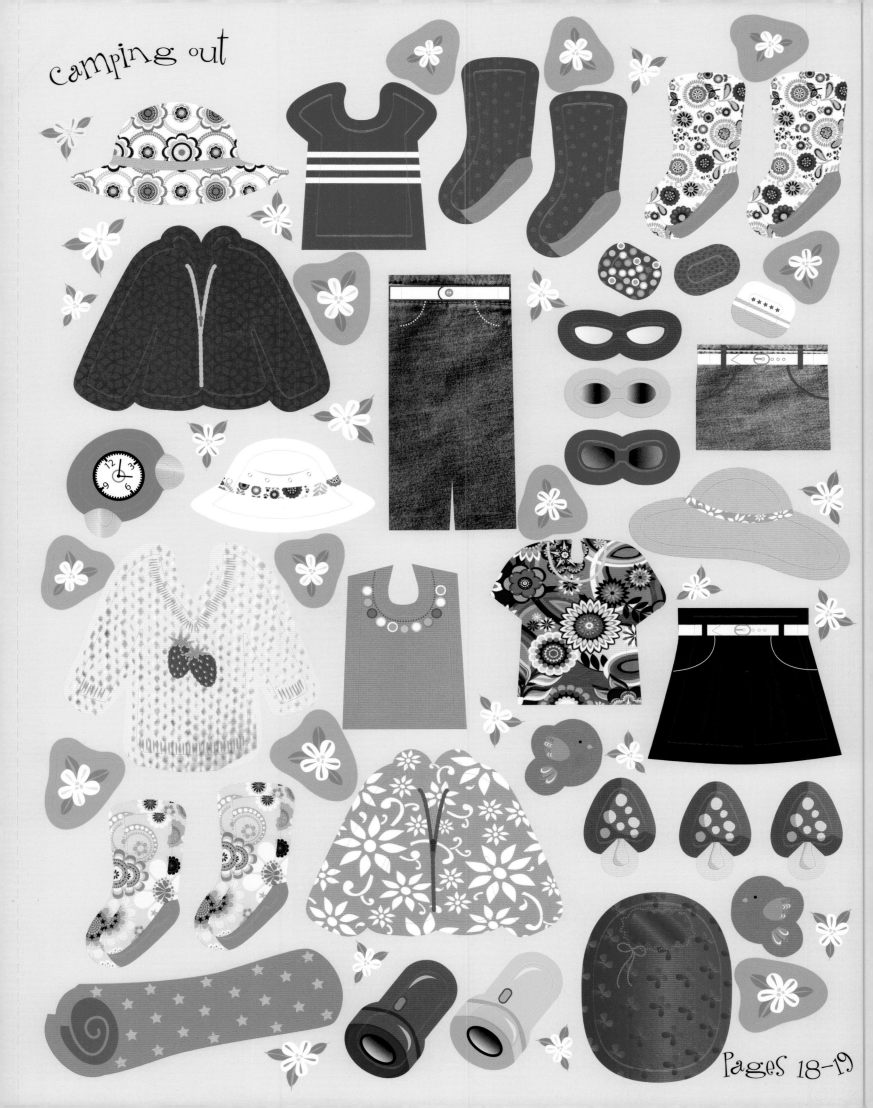

camping out

Visiting Venice

Pages 20-21

In the jungle

Pages 22-23

Photo album

* Tia by the sea *

* Chloé camping *

* Megan at the pyramids *

Page 24